W9-BRV-531

NOT SO FAST
SONGOLOLO

For my friend
Miriam Makalima

Other books by Niki Daly

Vim the Rag Mouse
Joseph's Other Red Sock

First Aladdin Paperbacks edition January 1996
Copyright © 1985 by Niki Daly
All rights reserved, including the right of reproduction in whole or in part in any form

Aladdin Paperbacks
An imprint of Simon & Schuster Children's Publishing Division
1230 Avenue of the Americas
New York, NY 10020

Also available in a Margaret K. McElderry Books edition
Printed in Hong Kong
10 9 8 7 6 5 4 3 2

Library of Congress Cataloging-in-Publication Data
Daly, Niki.
Not so fast, Songololo / written and illustrated by Niki Daly.—1st Aladdin Paperbacks ed.
p.   cm.
Summary: In South Africa, a young black boy shares a special day with
his grandmother when they go into the city on a shopping trip.
ISBN 0-689-80154-8
[1. Grandmothers—Fiction. 2. Shopping—Fiction.
3. Blacks—South Africa—Fiction. 4. South Africa—Fiction.] I Title.
PZ7.D1715 Nl   1996   [E]—dc20   94-40984

NOT SO FAST
SONGOLOLO

written & illustrated by
NIKI DALY

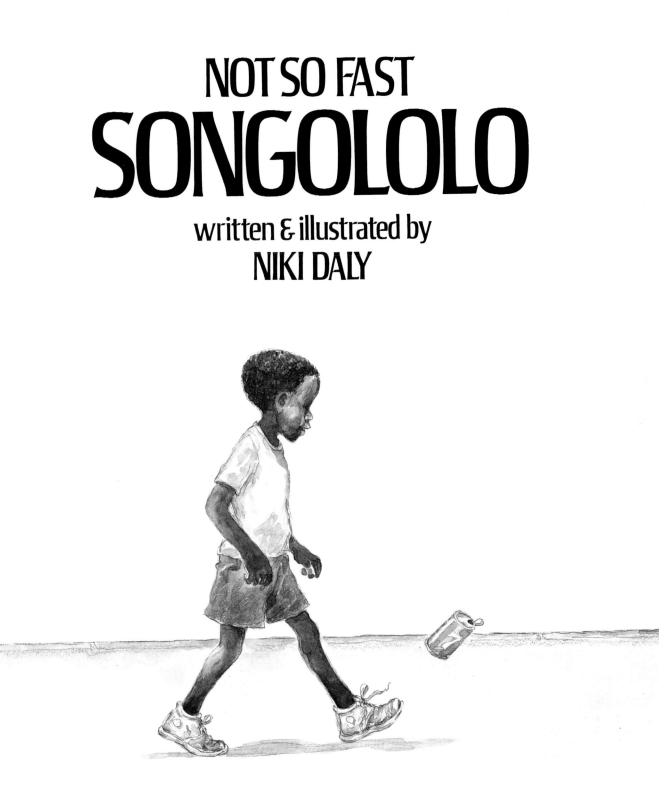

Aladdin Paperbacks

What a lot of noise!

"Weh, weh, weh!" Uzuti, the baby, was crying.

Adelaide was shouting, "Mongi, give me back my ballpoint pen."

Mama was calling, "Malusi, hurry up! Come on, Malusi."

Next door, Mr. Motiki's dog was barking at someone coming up the road.

Malusi liked doing things slowly.

He sang a little after he had pulled on his T-shirt.

He played a little and then he put on his shoes — his tackies.

They were very old tackies.

When they were new they had belonged to Mongi.

But now there were holes in them

and they belonged to Malusi.

Mr. Motiki's dog was still barking at someone
coming up the road.
Only an old person would walk so slowly.
She walked a little
and then stopped to lean on her stick for a while.
Mr. Motiki's dog had stopped barking.
Instead, he was wagging his tail.
It was okay. It was Gogo, Malusi's old granny, coming up the road.

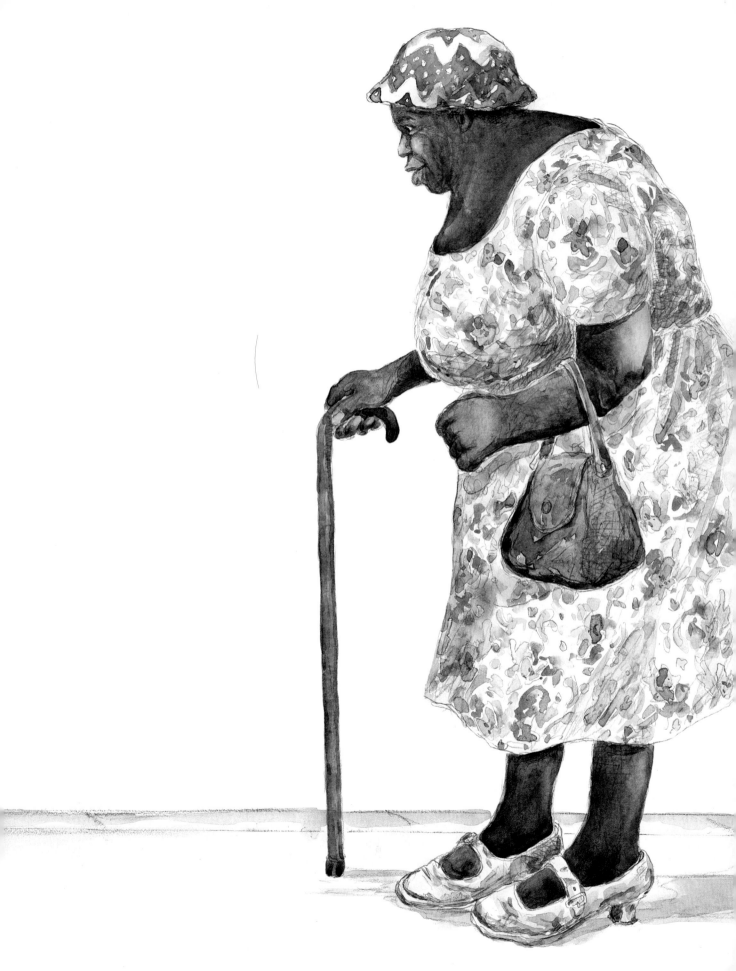

Gogo was old, but her face shone like new school shoes.
Her hands were large and used to hard work,
but they were gentle.
She rested her hands on Malusi's shoulders and said,
"I need someone to help me today."
Malusi kept quiet and listened carefully.
"I must do my shopping in the city. Yu! Those mad cars!
And the traffic lights! They mix me up," said Gogo.
Mama replied. "Okay, Malusi will go with you.
He is a big boy now."

Malusi liked doing things slowly.
So he walked a little, and then he stopped
to kick an old beer can.
Twang! The can danced down the street.
Gogo walked slowly behind.
"Haai!" Gogo sighed.
She was out of breath by the time they reached
the bus stop.

The beer can lay still
in the hot street.
When the bus came it squashed
the can flat.
That made Malusi laugh.

"Stop laughing and help me on to the
bus," scolded Gogo.
Malusi didn't know what he
should do —
push or pull his old Gogo.
She saw the worried look on his
face and laughed.
"Here, hold my stick. I'm
too old to kick a can
down the street. But I
can still climb
into a bus!"

The bus was full,
standing room only.
Malusi stayed close to Gogo.
She was wearing her best dress, and
he counted the colors in the pattern.
Red, green, pink,
blue, yellow and orange.
The bus stopped and some people climbed
out. Now Malusi and Gogo could sit down
next to the window.

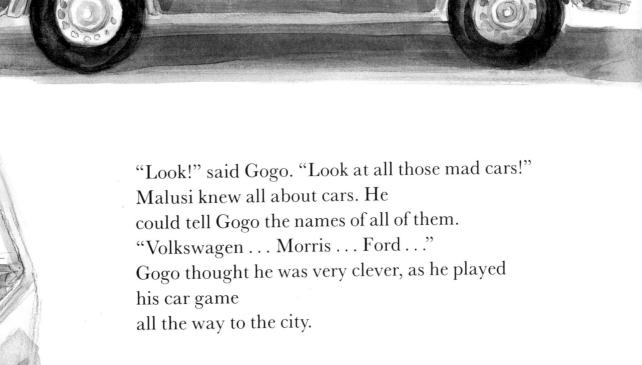

"Look!" said Gogo. "Look at all those mad cars!"
Malusi knew all about cars. He
could tell Gogo the names of all of them.
"Volkswagen . . . Morris . . . Ford . . ."
Gogo thought he was very clever, as he played
his car game
all the way to the city.

"Shu!" said Gogo. "So many people!"
Everyone was walking quickly.
Malusi walked ahead of Gogo.
Then he stopped and waited for her.
She looked older in the city, he thought.

Sometimes, while he was waiting for her,
he looked at all the things in the big shop windows.
There was a toy shop. And in the window a toy Volkswagen!

There was a shoe shop next. Tackies!
Malusi looked down at his old tackies
and then at the shoes in the window.
They were bright red with stripes down the side.
"What are you looking at?" asked Gogo, when
she caught up at last.
"Look, Gogo," said Malusi, "bright red tackies!"
Gogo looked at the new tackies
and then she looked at Malusi's old ones and she clicked her tongue.

Now they had to cross the busy road to reach OK Bazaars.
"There are those traffic lights!" shouted Malusi.
Gogo looked worried, so Malusi took her hand
and led her slowly over the crossing.
Just before they reached the other side,
the green light disappeared.
"Haai!" scolded Gogo.
"Those traffic lights mix me up!"

In the big store, Gogo looked at her shopping list.
She had to buy some groceries,
a new plastic tablecloth,
a mug and a bottle to keep beans in.
Everything cost a great deal.
Gogo kept her money in a little bag
pinned to the inside of her sleeve.
There it was always safe.

Soon it was time to cross the busy road again.
The light was green, so over they went.
They passed the flower seller
and the clothes shop.
Here was the shoe shop
with the bright red tackies looking so clean and new.
Malusi pressed his nose against the shop window
for a last look.
"Come along, Songololo!" called Gogo.
It was her special name for her grandson.

But instead of passing by the shoe shop,
Gogo went straight into it!
Malusi looked at Gogo's old shoes.
They were like worn-out tires on an old car.
"How much are those red tackies in the window?"
asked Gogo.
The man told her.
"Will you see if they fit the boy?" asked Gogo.
Malusi took off his old tackies and slowly
fitted his feet into the new ones.
The man pressed around his toes.
"They fit him very well," he said.
Malusi felt so happy that it hurt him
just to sit still.
He looked at Gogo and gave her a big smile.
"Shu!" said Gogo as she took out her money bag.
"One . . . two . . . three . . . four . . ." she counted.
"You can keep on your new tackies," Gogo told Malusi, so
he put his old ones into the new shoe box.

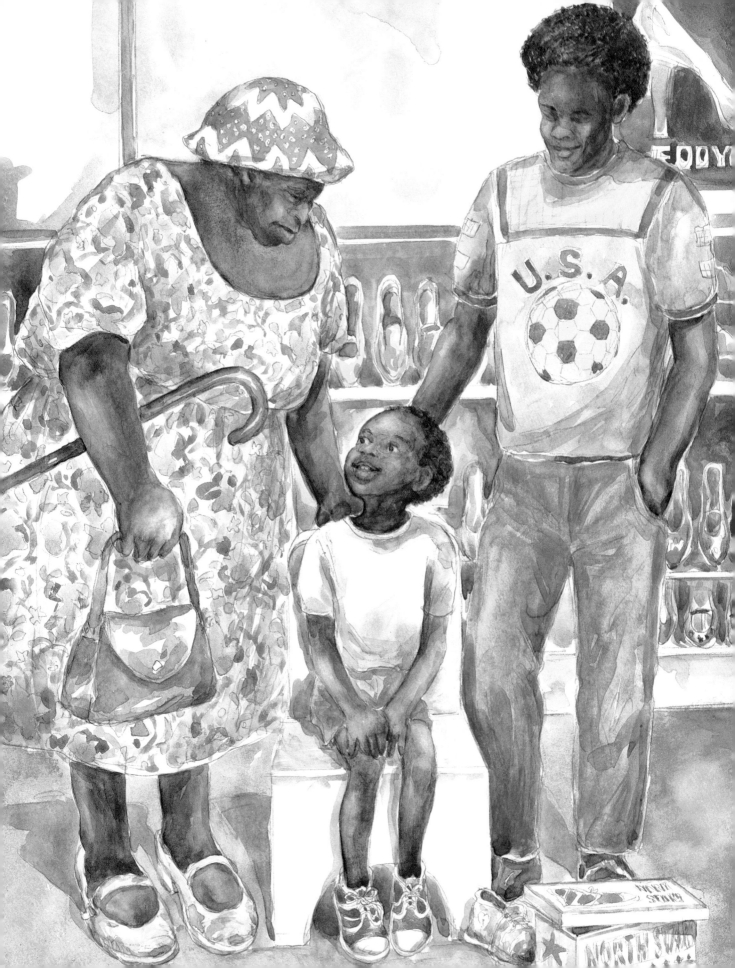

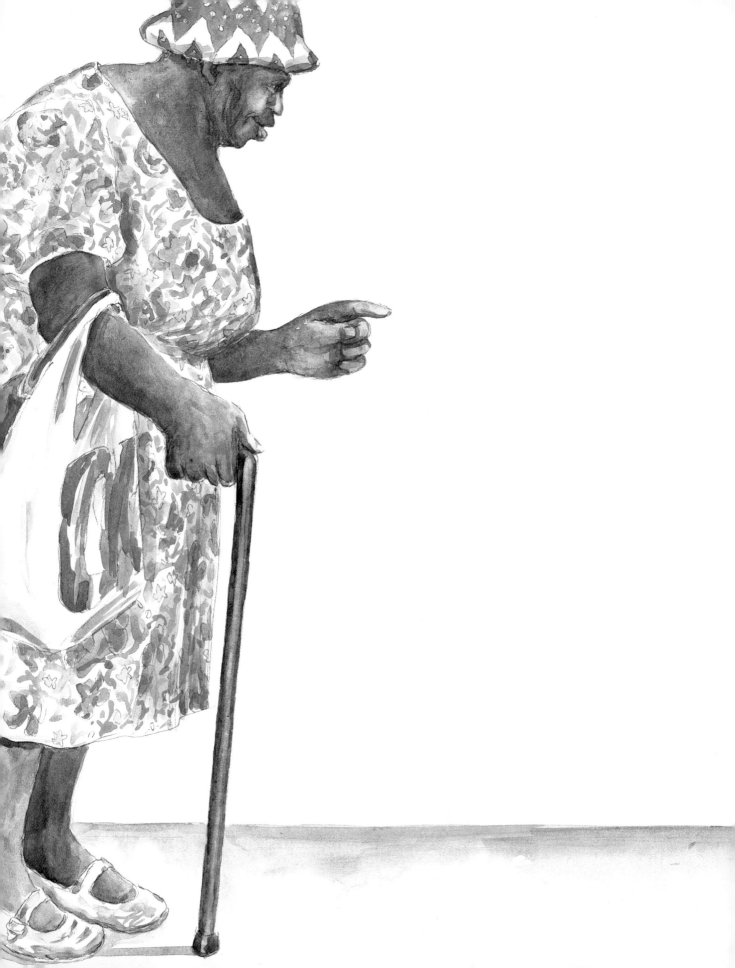

Malusi walked along proudly!
"Not so fast, Songololo!" called out Gogo.

At the bus terminal Gogo sat down to rest.
Malusi sat next to her with his feet up on the bench
so that he could look at his new tackies.
"You know, Gogo," Malusi said softly,
"these are very nice red tackies."

Gogo looked down at her own old shoes and said,
"Yes, maybe if I had red tackies with white stripes
I would also walk as fast as you."
Malusi looked at Gogo,
and then they both laughed.